YOLO
Juliet

💘

To Caroline and Michelle 😎,
for thinking of me 🤍

Text copyright © 2015 by Random House LLC

Image on page 21 copyright © Shutterstock/Odor Zsolt, page 72 copyright © Shutterstock/Nikolay Litov, page 86 copyright © Shutterstock/Patrik Ruzic

All rights reserved. Published in the United States by
Random House Children's Books, a division of Random House LLC,
a Penguin Random House Company, New York.

Random House and the colophon are registered trademarks of Random House LLC.

Emoji copyright © Apple Inc.

Visit us on the Web! randomhouseteens.com

Educators and librarians, for a variety of teaching tools,
visit us at RHTeachersLibrarians.com

Library of Congress Cataloging-in-Publication Data
is available upon request.
ISBN 978-0-553-53539-6 (trade) — ISBN 978-0-553-53548-8 (ebook)

MANUFACTURED IN CHINA
10 9 8 7 6 5 4 3 2
First Edition

YOLO
Juliet

william shakespeare

+

brett wright

Random House 🏠 New York

who's who

🧑 Romeo

🧔 Montague, Romeo's dad

🐶 Benvolio, Romeo's cousin

🏃 Balthasar, Romeo's servant

👧 Juliet

👴 Capulet, Juliet's dad

👩 Lady Capulet, Juliet's mom

🐱 Nurse, Juliet's nurse

🔪 Tybalt, Juliet's cousin

👑 The Prince of Verona

🇮🇹 Paris, the Prince's cousin

🐵 Mercutio, the Prince's cousin and Romeo's friend

⛪ Friar Laurence

⛪ Father John

👮 Chief Watchman

Send

characters you won't meet in this book

(aka people w/o smartphones)

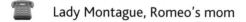

☎ Lady Montague, Romeo's mom

☎ Abram, Romeo's servant

☎ Petruchio, Tybalt's friend

☎ Sampson, servant

☎ Gregory, servant

☎ Peter, servant

☎ Paris's page

☎ Chorus

Act 1

[Scene 1]

Benvolio

Mornin', cuz! ☀️ You won't believe what just happened to me. 😨

I've already been in a fight! 💥❗💥

It's the Capulets again. They need to go! Especially Tybalt.

Hello? You there? I told your mom I'd see how you're doing. 😜

Romeo

What time is it? 🕐

Benvolio

Dude. It's <u>9 a.m.</u> Wake up! ⏰

Romeo

😞 Ugh, that's it? I don't wanna. I'm too depressed. I have nothing to live for. 😔

Benvolio

Oh, crap. 💩

Send

ROMEO

😕 What?

BENVOLIO

You're in 💘, aren't you?

ROMEO

Is it that obvious?

But she doesn't love me back. 💔

BENVOLIO

Cuz, here's the thing. Love sux.

I mean, on 📜 it sounds great. But feeling it?
No TY. 🙅

ROMEO

Tell me about it. But it has this sick control over me. 😫

I can't help it! Love is everything in the 🌏 —
awesome and stupid. Blech.

Anyway, sorry. What happened this morning? A fight?

Send

Benvolio

😔

Romeo

Why are you sad?

Benvolio

I'm bummed that you're bummed. 😕

Romeo

K, I can't handle this. You're just gonna make me feel worse. TTYL. ✌️

Benvolio

C'mon, wait! At least tell me who the girl is.

Romeo

Srsly?

She's hot, that's all you need to know. 🔥 Not just hot, but beautiful. And smart. 🤓 But she doesn't love me, so who cares? 🙁

Benvolio

Listen, just don't think about her anymore.

Send

ROMEO

WTF? How?

BENVOLIO

There are plenty of other 🐟 in the 🌊 dude.
Focus on someone else.

ROMEO

That's not gonna work. Other girls just make me think
about her more. I'm crazy. 🌀 🌀 I G2G. Bye. ✌️

[Scene 2]

PARIS

Sooo . . . whaddya think? 😃

CAPULET

About what?

PARIS

About me marrying your daughter! 👰

CAPULET

I told you. She's too young! 🔞 She's not even
fourteen yet. Ask me again in two years.

Send

paris

People younger than her get married all the time.

capulet

Yeah, and they also grow ⬆️ too fast. 🌱

But go ahead and ask her. If she says yes, you both have my blessing. 💒

paris

Yesss!

capulet

BTW, I'm having a party <u>tonight</u> at my 🏡. 🎉 🎈 You should come! There will be a lot of 👧 👧 👧 there, including my daughter. Maybe another one will catch your 👀. See you there!

📅 Event: 10+ People have been invited to Capulet's Mansion for Capulet's Dinner Party

- Signor Martino & his wife & daughters
- Mercutio & his brother Valentine
- Uncle Capulet & his wife & daughters
- Rosaline & Livia
- Signor Valentio & his cousin Tybalt

Send

ROMEO

Did you see the Capulet party that's happening <u>tonight</u>? We should go!

BENVOLIO

I did. And look who's gonna be there—Rosaline. 🌹 The "love of your life."

Let's sneak in and scope out the other hotties. I bet you'll change your tune 🎵 after we're on the scene. 🎬

ROMEO

NO one is better than Rosaline. But we're Montagues. We can't go to a party hosted by the Capulets. 🚫

BENVOLIO

Let's do it! I'll have serious FOMO if we don't go. 😜

Let's talk to Mercutio—he's on the list.

Besides, we're not going to start anything. We're going to make sure that Rosaline is worth all of this .

ROMEO

K, let's go! I can't wait to see her. 😍 L8R.

Send

[Scene 3]

Lady capulet

Juliet, honey, we need to talk. Love, Mom.

juliet

yeah, 👩 ?

Lady capulet

It's about 👰 . Love, Mom.

juliet

ugh, mom. noooo. 💁 i rly don't care about getting married right now. 💅

Lady capulet

You better start caring. I was already a mother by your age. Plenty of girls are finding husbands while you're still single. 👰👰👰💍 Love, Mom.

I'll just cut to the chase. A man named Paris 🇮🇹 has asked if he can marry you. 💍 He's a great option. I think you need to give him a chance. What do you think? Love, Mom.

Send

juliet

sigh. k, whatevz. i'll meet him. 😔 but i'm not promising anything.

Lady capulet

Oh, good! Now go get ready. Guests are starting to arrive for the party! Put on something cute. 👗 👠 💄
Love, Mom.

[Scene 4]

Group text: Romeo, Benvolio, Mercutio

Romeo

So, how are we going to do this? What's our excuse if we get caught?

Benvolio

You're thinking about this too much. We have our 🎭 on. No one will recognize us. We go in, we 💃, we 😘, and we exit. 🚪 Easy, breezy.

Romeo

I don't want to 💃. I'm still too 😔.

Send

mercutio

Can u stop being so sad n mopey 4 once? Ur a luvr, not a h8r. 💜 Get in there n prove it.

ROMEO

Yeah, well, this time my crush is actually crushing me. 👊

mercutio

U can't let this bring u ⬇️. Luv is the best thing in the 🌍.

ROMEO

Really? I hate love right now. 😠

mercutio

U gotta fight back, man. Show luv who's boss! 👮
We're wearing masks. We got protection.

Benvolio

Exactly, thaaank you. Let's go in already! I wanna shake it. 🎹 🎺 🎵

ROMEO

You guys go ahead. I'm gonna sit this one out. GL2U.

Besides, I don't think this is such a good idea. ☹️

Send

mercutio

Guh, Romeo! Y?

ROMEO

I had a dream last night.... 💭

mercutio

Gr8. 👍 Welcome 2 the club. So did I.

ROMEO

What was yours about?

mercutio

O, it was v informative. It told me that dreamers r liars. Ahem.

ROMEO

Yeah, lie in bed while they dream about the truth. 😴

mercutio

K, have u been dreaming about Queen Mab 👸 again?

ROMEO

IDEK who that is.

Send

Mercutio

U know, Queen Mab? The fairies' midwife.

K, she's super small. She travels in her little wagon each night n rides over men's noses. 👃👃 That's how she gets in2 their brains n makes them dream about—dun-dun-dun—luv! 🤍 She does all sorts of crazy stuff 2 people. Like sometimes she'll ride over girls' 👄 n then they'll start dreaming about kisses. But Queen Mab gives

Romeo

ENOUGH. I get it. You're messing with me. STFU. 😠

Mercutio

Ya, man. That's my point. Dreams r silly. 😛

Benvolio

Guys. GUYS. Hate to interrupt but this is taking forever. Dinner is probably over and by the time we get there it's going to be too late. ⌚

Send

Romeo

I don't want to get there on time anyway. I have a bad feeling about <u>tonight</u>. ☹️

But I'm outnumbered. Sigh. Let's go.

[Scene 5]

✅ Romeo has checked into Capulet's Mansion.

> **Romeo**
> At a party I'm not supposed to be at lol.
>
>   REPLY
>
> **Romeo:** Whoa! Spotted a hottie. She. Is.
> #PERFECT.
> **Tybalt:** 😡

● ● ●

Tybalt

What is our enemy doing here?!👀 This guy's definitely a Montague and he's staring at Juliet! 👧

Capulet

Is it Romeo?

Send

тʏʙalt

Yes! Disgusting Romeo! 😈

capulet

Calm down, it's NBD. He's harmless and from what I 👂 he's a good boy. You should be 😃 during this party, not 😔.

тʏʙalt

Not with him here. 👎

capulet

This is my 🏠 and you will get along with him tonight.

тʏʙalt

But he's making us look like idiots!

capulet

I won't let you ruin my party. Now go. And keep your mouth zipped . . . or else. 😬

тʏʙalt

Fine. I don't trust myself when I'm this 😠 anyway. But I'm not going to let Romeo get away with this.

Send

<u>Juliet direct message</u> –> with Romeo

hey. saw your update. was it abt me? here's my #. txt me!

ROMEO

Hi. 👋 You saw that? Sorry, I didn't think anyone even followed me. Thanks for your number. I wish I could come hold your hand, though.

JULIET

i know. me too. but we can't be seen together. 🚫

ROMEO

Why not? What if we found a corner to meet in?

JULIET

now? idk.

ROMEO

Really quickly. The one that's closest to you. Meet you there in a sec!

Send

Romeo

Just kissed the most beautiful girl in the room.
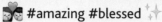 #amazing #blessed ✨

👍 Juliet likes this.   REPLY

Nurse: Uh. You know she's a Capulet, riiite?
#oohboy #thedrama
Romeo: !!!!! #aaahhh 😱

ROMEO

The girl I just kissed is a Capulet!!! 🙊 FML.
I just kissed my own enemy!!!

BENVOLIO

Let's GTFO! This party has peaked anyway. 🏃

ROMEO

I'm in serious trouble. 😟

● ● ●

NURSE

Girl, ya know what ya just did, rite?

Send

juliet

yeah, kissed the cutest boy in the room. i hope he's single. i'd rather 😵 than be with anyone else!

nurse

No, girl. I don't think ya understand. That boy is Romeo. 😎 He's a Mon-ta-gue.

juliet

are you freaking kidding me? great. i'm in 🤍 with the one person i can't be in love with. FML.

Send

Act 2

[Scene 1]

Benvolio

> Hey, have you seen Romeo? WTF, where did he go?

Mercutio

> Relax. He probs just went .

Benvolio

> No, he didn't. He ran away, I know it.

> Can you try texting him? 📱
> He won't answer mine.

Mercutio

> Ya, sure. NP.

Group text: Mercutio, Benvolio, Romeo

Mercutio

> Hey, lover boy. Come out, come out, wherever u are.
> We have Rosaline 🌹 here with us. . . .

Send

● ● ●

Benvolio

Cut it out! ✂️ If he finds out we're lying, he'll be pissed. 😠

Mercutio

Whatevz. I'm just trying 2 get him 2 show up. I'm tired n-e-way. 😴 Let's go.

Benvolio

Fine. No point in trying to find him if he doesn't want to be found.

[Scene 2]

✅ Romeo has checked into the Grounds Below Juliet's Balcony.

Send

Voice Memo from Romeo

<BACK **ROMEO** +

SMH. Sometimes my BFFs are so annoying. I just need to get away and have some alone time. Wait—what is that? 🔭· Holy crap. It's Juliet! She's so beautiful. She's brighter than the ☀. She's more gorgeous than the stars in the sky. 🌆 I want her so badly. I wish she knew how much. If only I could just reach out and touch her. 💂 It sounds like she's reading something. . . .

Send

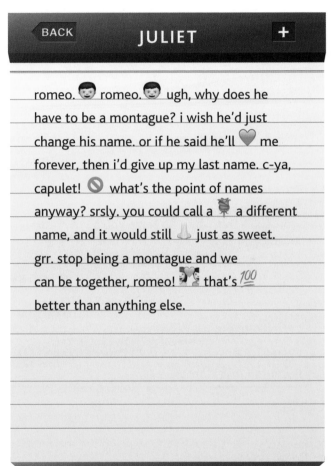

romeo. 👦 romeo. 👦 ugh, why does he have to be a montague? i wish he'd just change his name. or if he said he'll 💛 me forever, then i'd give up my last name. c-ya, capulet! 🚫 what's the point of names anyway? srsly. you could call a 🌹 a different name, and it would still 👃 just as sweet. grr. stop being a montague and we can be together, romeo! 👫 that's 💯 better than anything else.

Send

Voice Memo from Romeo

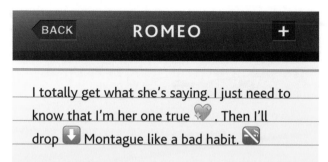

juliet

wait, romeo, is that you? 😨 have you been 👂 to me this whole time?

ROMEO

Maaaybe.

I want to show my face, but I know I shouldn't. Because I'm a Montague. 😖

juliet

no, keep texting. it's easier this way. you're too far down.

i don't want my family to 👂 you yelling. they'll be srsly upset. i'm talking, like, pissed. 😠

Send

how did you even get here? the walls around here are really high.

ROMEO

I scaled them, NBD. I couldn't wait to see you again!

And I'm not afraid of your family.

juliet

you should be. if they see you here, they'll kill you! 🔫

ROMEO

So what? That's nothing compared to being rejected by you. Chill. ❄️

juliet

sorry, it's just . . . i'd do anything to make sure they don't catch you.

ROMEO

Hello. I'm hidden in the dark. 🏙️ Plus, if you're not into me after all, then I'd rather be dead.

I can't live without you!

Send

juliet

srsly, how did you know where my bedroom was?

ROMEO

I just followed my 🖤. It led the way. 👣

juliet

it's a good thing it's dark. you're making me blush. 😊

listen, romeo. i really, really like you. i know i should have played hard-to-get, but i guess it's too late for that.

you heard me just now. i'm so into you. i mean . . .

i you, romeo.

ROMEO

Juliet, I swear on the 🌙

juliet

you swear on a piece of rock in the sky? um.

but the moon always changes. 🌙 🌑 🌕

Send

ROMEO

What should I swear on then?

JULIET

maybe we shouldn't make any promises yet. all of this happened as fast as ⚡.

we have a good thing going. 👍 let's see what happens the next time we meet.

i'm gonna go now. zzZ hope you sleep as well as i plan to. 😀

ROMEO

You're leaving me already??

JULIET

what else is there to say?

ROMEO

For starters, I'd be happy if we promised to 💜 each other forever. I'm talking, like, making it real. Like, married real.

Send

juliet

i've already poured my 🤍 out to you. i'd take it back if i could.

ROMEO

What the duck, Juliet!

The duck.

Ugh! Autocorrect. 😐

juliet

heehee. quack, quack. 🐣

ROMEO

WTF Juliet. Why would you say that ‼️

juliet

i'm just teasing. i mean i'd take it back so i could give it to you again and again. 😊 😉

i love you as deep as the ocean. 🌊 but i think i hear someone calling for me. hold on a sec. brb.

Send

Romeo

I wanna pinch myself. Am I dreaming or is this happening IRL? #truluv #blessed

 REPLY

juliet

okay, romeo. real quick. if you really, truly 🤍 me and want to get married . . .

let's chat tomorrow. sleep on it. 😴 we can figure out when and where to get married. but only if you really mean it.

sweet dreams!

what time 🕐 should i text you tomorrow?

ROMEO

Let's say 9. 🕐

juliet

perf! it's going to feel like years until then. 📅17

sorry i keep saying goodbye and then texting you again. i had a reason this time, i swear. i just forget.

Send

ROMEO

 That's okay. I'll stick around until you remember.

juliet

in that case, it might take me forever to remember what it was. hmm . . .

ROMEO

NP. Guess I found my new home right here.

juliet

i wish you didn't have to go.

but the sooner we go to bed, the sooner it's <u>tomorrow</u>. g'night!

ROMEO

Sweet dreams, you.

♫ Juliet is listening to Taylor Swift's "Love Story" on Renaissance FM

[Scene 3]

ROMEO

Morning, Friar Laurence!

Send

friar Laurence

Romeo, what are you doing up this early? You should be sleeping in. Have you even gone to bed, or have you been up all night? —FL

ROMEO

Er, the latter. I was having too great of a night to go to sleep! 😜

friar Laurence

Why? Were you with Rosaline? OMG, please forgive any sins you two might have committed. —FL

ROMEO

No way, Father! She's old news. 📰 I'm totally over her.

friar Laurence

Then where have you been? —FL

ROMEO

See, that's the thing. I've been with my enemy.

But I'm in 🤍 ! And so is she! And you're the only one who can help us.

Send

Friar Laurence

I'm confused. 😕 —FL

Romeo

I'm in love with Juliet Capulet.

I can tell you more later, but I need you to marry us. 💒 Today. It's urgent. 🚓

Friar Laurence

Holy 💩, Romeo! This came out of nowhere. You're over Rosaline that quickly? You could barely get out of bed, you were so sad. Now you're in love with someone else that you just met? Guess it's true: men love with their 👀 first. How do you know this won't happen again? —FL

Romeo

You're the one who was hard on me about Rosaline.

Friar Laurence

Because you were obsessed with her. But not because you loved her. There's a difference, IMHO. —FL

Romeo

You told me to forget about her! 👉

Send

Friar Laurence

I didn't mean by finding someone else! —FL

Romeo

You've got to understand. Rosaline never loved me. But Juliet does. She really does.

Friar Laurence

Ugh. Fine. 😤 Come with me. Let's plan this secret wedding. It may be the only thing that ends the hate between your two families anyway. 👨‍👨‍👦💥👨‍👨‍👦 —FL

[Scene 4]

Mercutio

Srsly, where's Romeo?

Benvolio

Got me. He didn't come 🏠 last night.

Mercutio

This is all Rosaline's fault. She's gonna lead him on until he goes legit insane. 🌀 Did I tell you I saw her on a dating app? I bet she's swiping right like mad. . . .

Send

Benvolio

I heard that Tybalt sent a letter to Romeo's father's house.

Mercutio

I bet he wants 2 fight.

Benvolio

Romeo will fight back, in that case.

Mercutio

Yup, he's a goner. He's already dead. Luv has killed him.

Do u think he stands a chance against Tybalt?

Benvolio

IDK. What's the 411 on Tybalt?

Mercutio

He's tough. 💪 Rly tough. He knows exactly what he's doing.

Let's just say I wouldn't want 2 be on the receiving end. He knows how 2 deliver a final blow to the 💀.

Send

Benvolio

Let's check in on Romeo.

Group text: Mercutio, Romeo, Benvolio

Mercutio

Bonjour, Romeo. Gotta admit, u faked us out pretty good last nite.

Romeo

Hey, guys. 🖐 What do you mean I faked you out?

Mercutio

Ya tricked us. U know wut I'm saying.

Romeo

Sorrrry. I had something really important to do.

Mercutio

Y'okay. "Important." 😉 😉

Romeo

That's one way of putting it.

Send

Mercutio

Out with it then! So how was her pink flower?

Benvolio

Ugh. Mercutio.

Romeo

Let's just say it's been pollinated.

Benvolio

Ugh. ROMEO!

Mercutio

Ha! Good 1.

Romeo

TY. But this joke is getting really bad.

Benvolio

Both of you are idiots. TTYL!

Send

Nurse

Sup, R.

Romeo

Who is this?

Nurse

Juliet's nurse. I got your digits from her. 📱
Hope that's cool.

Romeo

From Juliet?! Of course, in that case!

Nurse

Yeah, sooo, she wants me to tell you somethin',
but IDK if I should, tbh.

Romeo

You can trust me! Pinkie swear. Cross my 🤍 and hope
to die and stick a needle in my eye and all that.

I want to marry that girl! I plan to ask her ASAP. 👧

Send

nurse

K, relax. Dang.

I'll let her know you want to put a 💍 on it. Will that help?

ROMEO

Yes! But I need you to do me a huge favor.

Tell Juliet to sneak out of the house <u>this afternoon</u> and meet me at Friar Laurence's. Ask her to act like she has to go for confession. When she gets there, we can get married. I can pay you for your help. 💰

nurse

Aw, well, lookatchu, actin' all sweet. I can't take your 💰.

ROMEO

Take it!

nurse

Ya don't have to tell me twice! She'll see you <u>this afternoon</u>, bb.

Send

ROMEO

Wait! One more thing.

One of my friends will bring you a rope ladder.
I'll use it to climb over the walls at night.

NURSE

Wow, you're really into her, huh?

Weeelll, you should probs know that there's another
man after her. Paris. I think he's a QT, but Juliet
hates when I get all gushy. Plus, she just goes on and
on about you. Kinda annoying after a while, tbh. You
two are a match made in heaven. TT4N.

[Scene 5]

JULIET

omg. where are you??

what's taking so long?

were you able to find him?

you left at 9 and now it's noon. ugh! 🕘🕘🕘🕘

Send

nurse

Calm down, girl. I'm here.

juliet

FINALLY.so??

what happened? what's going on? what did he say?

nurse

Can ya hold your 🐴 🐴 for a sec? I'm beat. 💤 I've been 🏃 all over.

juliet

SRSLY? i need to know right away!

nurse

OMFG. I'm out of breath. 💨 Just give me a minute.

juliet

you're obvs not that tired if you're still texting.

c'mon! stop putting it off. is it bad news? is that why you won't tell me?

Send

nurse

Well, ya sure know how to pick 'em. That Romeo, he's cute. 😏

He's as gentle as a lamb. 🙇 Have ya had lunch yet?

juliet

no, not yet.

wait, don't change the subject. i already know all these things. did he say anything about marriage? 👰

nurse

Ugh, I have such a headache. My whole body hurts from running around all day for you. 👟 👟

juliet

ok ok. i'm sorry. i'll give you a foot and back rub when i see you next. 👣

now, did romeo say anything else?

nurse

Geez, all right. Maybe next time you should take care of your own stuff.

Send

juliet

i'm sorry. but i need to know. what did he say?

nurse

Can ya go to confession today? 🏛

juliet

yeah.

nurse

K, then get to Friar Laurence's. Ya got a future husband waiting there for you.

Meanwhile, I'll be setting up a ladder . . . or something . . . so he can visit you <u>tonight</u>. You get to have all the fun while I do the grunt work. 😤

juliet

omg. ty, ty, ty!!

nurse

Yeah, yeah. Hurry up and go.

juliet

on my way! wish me luck! 🍀

Send

[Scene 6]

ROMEO

> Guh, where is she? I can barely stand it. 😞

Friar Laurence

> Let's just hope we're doing the right thing. —FL

ROMEO

> Amen. 🙏 But whatever happens, it's fine. Nothing can destroy what I feel for this girl.

Friar Laurence

> Just slow your roll a bit, Romeo, okay? Everything in moderation. Don't too fast or too slowly. It's like eating a ton of honey. 🍯 It's sweet, but too much will make you sick. 😷 —FL

☑ Juliet has checked into Friar Laurence's Church.

Group text: Juliet, Romeo, Friar Laurence

JULIET

> good evening!!

Send

ROMEO

Ah! I'm so happy you're here. I can't wait to be married. If I love you this much now, I can only imagine what it'll be like when we're finally together forever. 🩶

JULIET

i know, right?! idek how to express what i feel! 😀

FRIAR LAURENCE

That's enough chitchat. Come with me. We have to do this quickly. ⛪ I'm not leaving you two alone until you're officially married. 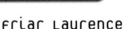 —FL

Send

Act 3

[Scene 1]

Benvolio

Let's call it a day, Mercutio. It's hot outside. ☀ And the Capulets are wandering around. I don't want to run into them and get into a fight. Heat makes people 😠.

Mercutio

Oh, plz, Ben. Ur one of those guys who has a sword but never uses it. 🗡 N then u pull it out 4 no reason at all.

Benvolio

Nuh-uh. 🙁 Am I really?

Mercutio

U get 😠 at the smallest things. N yet ur the one telling me about restraint? 🚫 Y'okay.

Benvolio

Ugh, hold on. The Capulets are texting me. 😦

Mercutio

IDGAF. 😐

Send

Group text: Benvolio, Mercutio, Tybalt

Benvolio

Adding Mercutio here.

Mercutio

Wut is it, Ty?

Tybalt

Good afternoon, boys. I'd like to have a word with you.

Mercutio

Psh. Just 1?

Tybalt

😒 Mercutio, you hang out with Romeo, right?

Mercutio

Hang out? Like we're in a band?

Benvolio

Do we have to talk about this now? 👀 Maybe we should meet in person.

Send

TYBALT

Yes, we have to talk about it. In fact, let's get Romeo in on this.

Group text: Tybalt, Mercutio, Benvolio, Romeo

TYBALT

Romeo, there's only one thing I can call you: a villain. 😾

ROMEO

Tybalt, I'm not even gonna sweat that. 💦 I have a reason to like you now. Plus, it's obvs you don't know me at all.

TYBALT

That doesn't excuse what you've done to me. We're fighting this afternoon. Meet me on the streets. 🔪

ROMEO

I haven't done anything to you. And I 🤍 you now— I just can't tell you why yet. Let's not fight.

MERCUTIO

Romeo, wut r u doing? Y r u backing down from him? If u won't fight him, I will. 🔪

Send

TYBALT

What do you want from me? 😤

MERCUTIO

2 fight u. Now.

Ty, hurry up n draw ur sword.

TYBALT

Fine. If that's what you want, that's what you get. 🔪

ROMEO

Mercutio, stop! 🚫 What are you doing? Ben, we've got to stop them. Fighting in the streets is banned here. Stop it, you guys! 😟

✅ Mercutio, Tybalt, Benvolio, and Romeo have checked into the Streets of Verona.

Group text: Mercutio, Romeo, Benvolio

MERCUTIO

Romeo. Where are you? I'm hurt. 😟 His sword got me. Did Ty get away ⁉️

Send

Benvolio

What? You're hurt? 😭

Mercutio

I just need 2 see a doctor, that's all. 🏥

Romeo

Okay. Be brave. 💪

Mercutio

It's not deep, but it hurts like a mofo. 😔 I'll b a goner by 2morrow. 💀

Ugh, I can't believe it was Ty who killed me. I hope a plague curses his 🏠. Y did u try to stop us, Romeo?

Romeo

IDK. 😞 I thought it was the right thing to do.

Mercutio

Ben, take me inside somewhere. This is the end.

I hope a plague curses both of ur houses, Romeo.

Send

Romeo

Omg. OMFG. Mercutio was killed defending me! WTF! #RIP

 REPLY

Benvolio

 Mercutio is dead. He's in Heaven now.

ROMEO

This is very bad, Ben. The future is bleak.

Group text: Benvolio, Romeo, Tybalt

Benvolio

OMG. Tybalt, you suck!

ROMEO

You're alive . . . and Mercutio is dead. I dare you to call me a villain again, Tybalt. Do it and you'll join Mercutio in Heaven.

Send

TYBALT

It's you who will be joining him next.

 Romeo
Just got Tybalt. That's what you get for killing my cousin.

👍 Benvolio likes this.   REPLY

Benvolio: Romeo! You have to get out of here. 🏃 You'll be put to death.

Group text: The Prince, Benvolio, Lady Capulet, Montague

THE PRINCE

Just saw Romeo's status update. Is it true? He killed Tybalt? 😠

BENVOLIO

It was insanity, Prince. 🌀 Tybalt killed Mercutio. Then Romeo killed Tybalt. 😔

LADY CAPULET

What! 😢 Tybalt was my nephew. This can't—this can't be happening. Prince, you have to take revenge. You have to kill someone from the Montague family. Angrily, LC.

Send

The Prince

Ben, who started this fight?

Benvolio

Tybalt did. Romeo tried to talk him down, but Tybalt stabbed Mercutio.

Something snapped in Romeo. He killed Tybalt too.

I tried to break it up, but it was no use! 😫

Lady Capulet

Ben is a Montague. He's lying. 👉 The Montagues jumped Tybalt and killed him. Prince, you know that Romeo must die. Grr, LC.

The Prince

So if Romeo killed Tybalt, and Tybalt killed Mercutio, then who should pay for Mercutio's life?

Montague

Not Romeo. He was only avenging his friend.

Send

The Prince

Then I have no choice but to kick Romeo out of Verona. And now you've gotten me involved in your rivalry.

Mercutio was my family. I'll punish you all for this. There's no use 😭 or begging. Tell Romeo to leave immediately or else he'll be joining Mercutio and Tybalt . . . in the grave. 💀

[Scene 2]

Nurse

Girl, I got some bad news. 😔

Juliet

what is it??

Nurse

He's dead. 💀

Juliet

WHO?? ROMEO?!

Send

nurse

It was bad. I saw it with my own 👀. He's gone. Dead as a doornail.

juliet

omg. plz not romeo. plz! 😭

nurse

No, girl. It's Tybalt. Romeo killed him and now Romeo's been exiled, oof.

juliet

are you kidding me? did romeo do it? did he kill tybalt?

nurse

Yeah. 😞

juliet

i can't believe it. how could i have ever trusted him? i'm a fool! 😭

nurse

That's 'cause all men are 🐷 🐷 🐷, girl. Ya can't trust any of 'em.

Send

juliet

don't say that about romeo. he's not a 🐶, i swear.

nurse

Say what? Now you're going to DEFEND him? Did you hear what I just said? He killed your cousin.

juliet

i know what he did, but he's my husband. i think i'm allowed to be confused right now, k? ☹️

nurse

Try to have a little perspective, hon.

juliet

try to have some compassion, hon! 😭 nothing will make me feel better until i see romeo again.

nurse

Okay, okay, quit cryin', girl. I know where he is. I'll go find him for you.

juliet

you will?? THANK YOU! here, give him my 💍. and tell him to hurry!

Send

[Scene 3]

✅ Romeo has checked into Friar Laurence's Church.

Friar Laurence

You here, Romeo? —FL

Romeo

Yes, I'm hiding out. What's going to happen to me?
Am I going to die?

Friar Laurence

You're being exiled from Verona. —FL

Romeo

That's worse than death!

Friar Laurence

Really? You killed someone! —FL

Romeo

It is worse! It means I'll never see Juliet again.

Send

Friar Laurence

You're being overdramatic. —FL

Romeo

Ugh. You just don't understand.

☑ Nurse has checked into Friar Laurence's Church.

Group text: Romeo, Nurse, Friar Laurence

Romeo

Nurse!! 😃

Nurse

R? Wait . . . why are we texting?

Romeo

I can't be heard talking about Juliet. How is she?
Does she hate me? What did she say?

Nurse

Boy, she's just crying and crying. And keeps asking for ya.

Romeo

OMG, what have I done? I want to die. 🗡️

Send

Friar Laurence

SNAP OUT OF IT! 😡 You can't kill yourself.
Nurse, tell Juliet that Romeo is on his way. —FL

Nurse

I'll go right now. R, she wanted me to give you
something. 💍 Leaving it here for you. TT4N!

Romeo

Her ring! I feel so much better.

Friar Laurence

You better go now. Don't waste time. 🕐 —FL

[Scene 4]

Group text: Paris, Capulet, Lady Capulet

Paris

Any luck yet with Juliet? 🤍

Capulet

I'm sorry, Paris, but we've been a little busy lately.

Send

paris

NP. I understand. With Tybalt dead and all that.

K, good night. Tell Juliet I say hello.

lady capulet

Of course, Paris. 📖 I'll talk to her <u>tomorrow</u>. She's locked herself in her room right now. Love, LC.

capulet

Don't worry. Juliet will do what her father says.

Can you be ready to marry her in three days? 💒

paris

Absolutely! 😃

capulet

It's settled then. We'll talk to her in the meantime. See you later!

Send

[Scene 5]

✅ Romeo has checked into the Grounds Below Juliet's Balcony.

ROMEO

Juliet, <u>tonight</u> was great. But it's morning. 🌄 So I'm leaving before I get killed.

JULIET

no! don't go yet. plz. it's not quite daylight.

ROMEO

You're right. I'm coming back. I never want the night to end.

JULIET

me neither. 😔

⬤ ⬤ ⬤

NURSE

J! Your 👵 is coming to check on you! You in danger, girl.

⬤ ⬤ ⬤

Send

juliet

shoot. you've got to get going. my mom is on her way. ttyl! 😚

Romeo

Okay. Juliet! Even though things are crazy 🌀 now, think of all the stories we'll have to tell later on. TTYS! 😚

● ● ●

Lady capulet

Yoo-hoo! Juliet, you awake? Love, Mom.

juliet

mooom. i don't feel so well. 😩 😔

Lady capulet

Oh, honey. Are you going to stay in there and cry forever? Your tears won't bring Tybalt back. Love, Mom.

juliet

easy for you to say. i can't stop crying.

Send

Lady Capulet

Are you crying for your cousin? Or are you really crying for that horrible Romeo? Love, Mom.

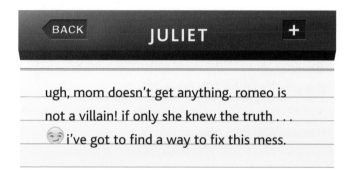

BACK **JULIET** +

ugh, mom doesn't get anything. romeo is not a villain! if only she knew the truth . . . 😏 i've got to find a way to fix this mess.

Juliet

gee, mom, you're right. he is horrible. i wish i could make everything right.

Lady Capulet

Don't worry, sweetie. Your mom is on top of it. 😉 I plan on sending someone to find Romeo and poison his drink. We'll finally have justice. Love, Mom.

And . . . more good news! 😃 Your father has arranged for you to marry Paris 🇮🇹 in three days! Isn't that wonderful?! Love, Mom.

Send

juliet

mom, how can i marry someone i don't even know?

tell dad to forget it.

Lady capulet

Why don't you tell him yourself, in that case?
We'll get the Nurse too. Love, Mom.

Group text: Lady Capulet, Juliet, Capulet, Nurse

Lady capulet

I told your daughter your news and, well, Juliet, why
don't you tell him what you told me. Love, LC.

juliet

i won't marry paris. it's as simple as that.

capulet

Excuse me? Aren't you happy about this match?
Aren't you thankful? There's no better man you
could possibly marry!

Send

juliet

i am NOT happy or thankful for any of this. i WON'T marry him. 🙅‍♀️

capulet

You will be at the church in three days to marry Paris. And that! is! final, young lady!

juliet

plz, i am begging you, dad! do not make me do this. 🙏

capulet

I can't even talk to you anymore. I'm so disappointed in you. 😞 I can't believe we're even related.

nurse

Hey now! Ya shouldn't say that to your own flesh and blood.

capulet

You stay out of this! It's none of your GD business.

nurse

Oh, excuse me? 😨 I think I'm allowed to speak my mind.

Send

capulet

Save it for later. No one is interested in what you have to say.

Lady capulet

Dear! I think you better watch your temper. You know what it does to your blood pressure. Love, LC.

capulet

Well, dear, I'm angry! 😠 Paris is a perfect match for her. And either you marry him, Juliet, or you can forget you even have a family. I don't care where you go or what happens to you. But you're not welcome here. 😡 Choose wisely.

Group text: Juliet, Lady Capulet, Nurse

juliet

this is so unfair! 😭

Lady capulet

I'm sorry, but I agree with your father. It's up to you to figure it out. Love, Mom.

Send

juliet

omg. nurse, what am i going to do?? 😟

romeo is out there and they want me to go through with this!

nurse

Listen, girl. I know ya married Romeo.

But he doesn't even live here anymore. He's as good as dead. Maybe you should look into Paris. At least you can actually, ya know, see him.

juliet

you really mean that?

nurse

Yeah, J. I do.

juliet

i guess i see your point.

k, tell mom i'm going to friar laurence's. i need to ask for major forgiveness. 🙏

Send

Act 4

[Scene 1]

Paris

> Thursday it is for the wedding!

Friar Laurence

> But that's so soon. 😦 —FL

Paris

> Capulet wants what he wants.

> It's Juliet, you see. She's been crying nonstop over Tybalt's death. 😭 Her father wants us to get married so she'll be happy again. 😃

Group text: Paris, Juliet, Friar Laurence

Paris

> Hey there, Juliet! Adding you to this convo, my wife.

Juliet

> we aren't married, paris.

Send

Friar Laurence

> I should talk to Juliet. Paris, could you leave us alone? —FL

Paris

Of course. I don't want to interfere.

See you on Thursday, my love.

● ● ●

Juliet

oh, thank you for getting rid of him. father, i'm miserable! 😭

Friar Laurence

> I know, I know. I heard that nothing can stop what's happening on Thursday. —FL

Juliet

there must be something you can do. plz? otherwise i'm going to solve this the only way i know how. . . . ✒

i'd rather die than marry paris.

Send

Friar Laurence

Stop! Killing yourself is a little drastic. —FL

💡 But drastic might be what we need right now. —FL

Juliet

anything! just tell me the plan. 😀

Friar Laurence

Here's the deal: Go to your and tell everyone that you're happy to marry Paris. Tomorrow is Wednesday, so make sure you're alone tomorrow night. 🌙 Don't let anyone stay with you, not even your nurse. —FL

I'm sending you a vial. —FL

Send

> When you're in bed, mix the contents of the vial and drink it. —FL

> The potion will make it look like you're dead, but you'll actually just sleep for about forty-two hours. When they discover you in the morning, they'll prepare you for burial in your family's tomb. Meanwhile, I'll send Romeo there to wait for you to wake up. Sound good? —FL

juliet

> yes! i'm ready. 👍

> love will get me through this. 🖤🤍🖤

[Scene 2]

juliet

> dad, you there?

capulet

> What is it? Where have you been?

Send

juliet

i went to see friar laurence.

i'm so sorry. i realize that i've been acting selfish. 👧 from now on, i'm going to do whatever you say. i promise.

that includes marrying paris. 🇫🇷

capulet

You mean it? This is great news! 😃

In that case, let's move the wedding up to tomorrow! 💑 Bless Friar Laurence for talking some sense into you.

juliet

i'm going to pick out a dress with nurse now. 👰 ttyl.

● ● ●

capulet

Great news, dear! Juliet is finally listening to us. I'm going to move the wedding up to tomorrow.

Send

Lady capulet

Tomorrow, really? But how will we ever have everything ready by then? Love, LC.

capulet

Don't worry about a thing. I've got it all figured out. 💡

Go get some sleep. 😴 I'm going to find Paris and tell him the good news. I can't wait! 👏

[Scene 3]

Lady capulet

Juliet, honey, do you need help picking out your clothes? 👱 Love, Mom.

juliet

no thanks. i got it covered.

if it's okay, i'd like to be alone. i'm sure you've got a lot of stuff to plan for tomorrow anyway. 🎉 🎁

Lady capulet

Okay, sweetie! Get some rest. zᶻᶻ Love, Mom.

Send

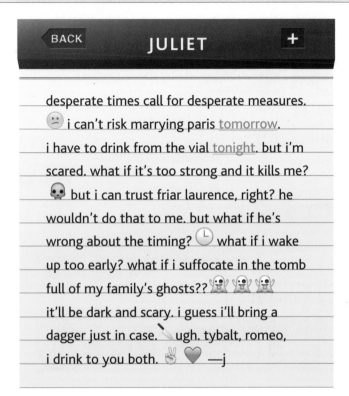

JULIET

desperate times call for desperate measures. 🙁 i can't risk marrying paris <u>tomorrow</u>. i have to drink from the vial <u>tonight</u>. but i'm scared. what if it's too strong and it kills me? 💀 but i can trust friar laurence, right? he wouldn't do that to me. but what if he's wrong about the timing? 🕐 what if i wake up too early? what if i suffocate in the tomb full of my family's ghosts?? 👻 👻 👻 it'll be dark and scary. i guess i'll bring a dagger just in case. 🗡 ugh. tybalt, romeo, i drink to you both. ✌️ 💚 —j

[Scene 4]

Group text: Lady Capulet, Capulet, Nurse, Paris

Lady Capulet

Ooh, we're so close to being ready! 💃 Nurse, we need some more spices for the food. Love, LC.

Send

nurse

Sure thing. We need more 🍩 🍩 too.

capulet

Hurry, everyone! We don't have much time left. We need more 🍗 too!

nurse

What ya need is to get some sleep, mister. You've been up all night. You're gonna end up sick! 😷

capulet

Psh! I've stayed up longer for less important things before and have never gotten sick. 😛

Lady capulet

She's right, dear. You really should rest up. Love, LC.

capulet

Nonsense. Nurse, make yourself useful and go wake Juliet. 👧 It's almost time. I'll go get Paris. 📖 This is so exciting! 🎎

Send

[Scene 5]

✅ Nurse has checked into Juliet's Chambers.

nurse

> Yoo-hoo! Hey, J. Time to wake up, girl.

> Ya up yet? Ya get enough beauty rest?

> Girl, srsly. It's time to get up.

> K, I'm coming in. Ya better be decent.

 Nurse
I guess some people sleep in the same clothes they wore yesterday. Nasty!

👍   REPLY

Nurse: Oh ! J is dead!
Lady Capulet: What are you talking about? —LC.
Nurse: Srsly. J won't wake up.
Lady Capulet: Oh, no! We need her father here, now. 😭😭 —LC.

● ● ●

Send

capulet

Where are you? Paris is waiting. 📖

Lady capulet

It's Juliet. OMG. Our daughter is dead. 😭 Sadly, LC.

capulet

No, she can't be. Let me see her.

✅ Capulet has checked into Juliet's Chambers.

capulet

She's so cold. ❄️ Her blood has stopped. 😔

She's gone. Oh, Juliet. 😭

Group text: Friar Laurence, Paris, Capulet, Lady Capulet, Nurse

Friar Laurence

Hello, everyone. Is the bride ready to go to ? —FL

capulet

Our beautiful is . . . dead.

Send

paris

She can't be! I've waited all my life for this morning.

Lady capulet

I only had one daughter! One! And now she's dead. 💀 This is the worst day of my life. Mourning, LC.

Nurse

Today is like one giant black hole. ⚫

capulet

We have to bury her. Along with whatever happiness we have left.

friar Laurence

Everyone relax. She's in a better place now. —FL

capulet

🤮 We planned a wedding . . . and now it's a funeral.

friar Laurence

Come on, people. We have to prepare for burial. It's the right thing to do. Let's go. I'm so sorry for our tragic loss. —FL

Send

Act 5

[Scene 1]

Balthasar

Hi.

Romeo

Who is this? 😕

Balthasar

It's me, Balthasar.

Romeo

Oh, sorry. Didn't recognize the number.

Balthasar

I upgraded to the newest model. New me, new number.

Romeo

That's nice.

What's going on? Do you have news from Verona? How's Juliet? 👧

Send

вalthasar

TBH, not so good. 😔

ROMEO

What do you mean?!

вalthasar

Juliet is dead, Romeo. I'm really sorry. She's being buried in her family's tomb.

ROMEO

NO! I can't believe it. 😭

Balthasar, bring me a . I'm going to Verona tonight. I have to. Meet me in a few. I've got an errand to run.

вalthasar

You got it.

Romeo

Just purchased the deadliest poison available online. 🍷 Here goes nothing. #gulp

                    REPLY

Send

[Scene 2]

Friar Laurence

Were you able to deliver the letter I wrote to Romeo?? 📬 —FL

Father John

OOF, BAD NEWS.

SO I WENT TO FIND ONE OF OUR BROTHERS SO HE COULD COME WITH ME BECAUSE I DIDN'T WANT TO GO ALONE. (HE WAS VISITING WITH THE SICK. 😷)

Friar Laurence

Why are you yelling? —FL

Father John

I DON'T KNOW WHAT YOU MEAN.

Friar Laurence

You mad? —FL

Send

father john

WHAT? NO. I DON'T KNOW HOW TO TURN CAPS OFF.

friar Laurence

Okay, okay, keep going. —FL

father john

TURNS OUT, THE HOUSE HE WAS IN HAD THE PLAGUE! OOPS! HEHE.

WE WERE QUARANTINED INSIDE AND I COULDN'T LEAVE. 🤦 SO THE LETTER NEVER REACHED ROMEO. SORRY!!

friar Laurence

Holy 💩 ! —FL

That letter was very important! 😖 —FL

I need to get to the tomb right away. —FL

[Scene 3]

✅ Paris has checked into Juliet's Tomb.

Send

Paris

 Juliet, I can't believe you were taken so soon. I brought you flowers for your grave. I'll water them every day. Probably with my tears. 😭

👍 REPLY

Romeo

I have everything I need to get into Juliet's tomb. I'm as ready as I'll ever be. I must see her face one more time. I gave Balthasar a 📝 to deliver to my father that explains everything. Nothing will stand in my way!

👍 REPLY

Paris: Dude, I'm already here.

You are a 😈. You've got to be stopped.
Romeo: Stop being so dramatic. I'm coming there to die. 🍷
Paris: Psh. 😠 Right. If you come here, I will not let you escape.

Send

✅ Romeo has checked into Juliet's Tomb.

🏛 Paris

Ugh. Romeo got me. 🔪 #dying Please let me lie next to Juliet forever. RIP, me. 💀

👍 REPLY

Romeo: I'm only letting you lie next to Juliet because there's been too much death and you deserve a proper burial.

📣 Voice Memo from Romeo

I'm nervous to open the tomb. . . . 💥 Oh, Juliet. I see you. 👀 I see your beautiful face. 👧 You've brought so much light to this dark grave. Suddenly I feel . . . happy. 😄 No, that can't be right. I don't understand it. 😕 I've heard that some men are relieved right before they die, but it feels wrong knowing all the death I've caused. Poor Tybalt. Juliet, you're perfect. I'm so sorry

Send

for everything. But now I can be with you forever. I will rest with you for eternity. With this kiss, I will join you. 😘 And now . . . the poison. 🍷 So I can die with a kiss. RIP, me. . . .

✅ Friar Laurence has checked into Juliet's Tomb.

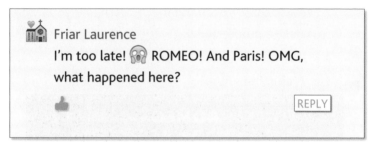

🏛️💖✝️ **Friar Laurence**
I'm too late! 🙀 ROMEO! And Paris! OMG, what happened here?

👍   REPLY

✅ Friar Laurence has checked out of Juliet's Tomb.

juliet

yawn. friar laurence, i'm awake. 😄 where's romeo? i did everything you told me to do! everything should work out now, right?

Send

Friar Laurence

Juliet, there's no time to talk. I'm outside your tomb.
I hear someone coming.●●We have to go. Romeo is dead,
and so is Paris. You're not safe here. Come with me. —FL

Juliet

what??!! are you crazy? i can't leave if
that's true. go without me.

 Voice Memo from Juliet

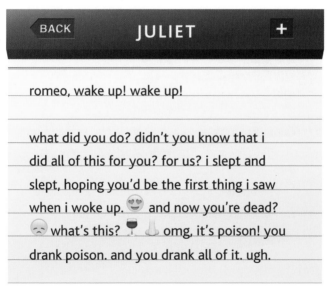

> ◁ BACK **JULIET** +
>
> romeo, wake up! wake up!
>
> what did you do? didn't you know that i
> did all of this for you? for us? i slept and
> slept, hoping you'd be the first thing i saw
> when i woke up. 😍 and now you're dead?
> 🙁 what's this? 🍷 👃 omg, it's poison! you
> drank poison. and you drank all of it. ugh.

Send

maybe there's still some left on your and if i just kiss you . . . 🥰

nothing. wtf! fine. then i'm gonna use this instead. goodbye, cruel 🌍 . and see you soon, my romeo. 🥰 rip, j . . .

✅ The Prince has checked into Juliet's Tomb.

👑 **The Prince**
What is going on around here? So much noise and commotion! Hmph. 😤

👍   REPLY

Capulet: I was just about to ask the same thing. I'm heading over there now.
👍 Lady Capulet likes this

Lady Capulet: Everyone is running around the tomb! I can hear people shouting, "Juliet!" "Romeo!" "Paris!" Confused, LC.

Send

✅ Chief Watchman has checked into Juliet's Tomb.

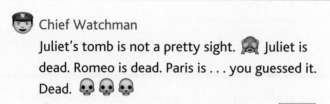

Chief Watchman
Juliet's tomb is not a pretty sight. 🙈 Juliet is
dead. Romeo is dead. Paris is . . . you guessed it.
Dead. 💀 💀 💀

👍 | REPLY |

The Prince: How could this happen? All three?
I want answers!
Chief Watchman: I'm still investigating. But
there are tools on the ground that could have
opened the tomb. 🔨 🔧

✅ Capulet has checked into Juliet's Tomb.

capulet

OMG. Juliet stabbed herself with that 🗡 .
That should be in Romeo's back! 😠

Lady capulet

😭 😭 😭 —LC

● ● ●

Send

THE PRINCE

I've got some bad news.

MONTAGUE

😌 My wife died last night. She couldn't take Romeo's exile any longer. You mean there's more bad news?

THE PRINCE

Did you see the Watchman's status? 🙁

MONTAGUE

Hold on.

Oh, Romeo. You idiot. I'm supposed to die first!

THE PRINCE

We need to figure out what happened. 😟
Let's speak with Friar Laurence. I'll loop us all in.

Group text: The Prince, Friar Laurence, Montague, Capulet

THE PRINCE

Hey, FL. Mind explaining what happened?

Send

Friar Laurence

😟 I don't think I'll live long after confessing this, but . . . here goes. —FL

I married Romeo and Juliet in secret. 👰 It was on the same day that Romeo was banished. Juliet cried nonstop because she missed Romeo, not Tybalt. Then someone had the bright idea 💡 to cure her sadness by making her marry Paris 🔲🔲. She came to me, threatening to take her own life if I didn't help. So I gave her a sleeping potion. ᶻᶻ She'd look dead to everyone else, but she'd wake up in time to reunite with Romeo. At least, that was the idea. —FL

I wrote a letter 📝 to Romeo telling him exactly when to come to the tomb, but it never reached him. I ran 🏃 here, and by the time I arrived, Romeo and Paris were already dead. Juliet woke up, but I heard a noise, got scared, and ran. 👻 The sight of it all must have been too much for her to bear. That's when she picked up the 🗡 and . . . oh, this is what it's come to. —FL

Send

The Prince

Did you get all of that? Capulet? Montague?

Look what your family feud has caused! 😠

You've lost your only children. And because I looked the other way, I lost family too. We've ALL been punished for this.

Capulet

OMG. Montague, I'm so sorry. I don't know what else to say right now. This is all too horrible. 😔

Montague

FML. I know. I can't believe we let this happen. We are so stupid. 😖

The Prince

I think it's safe to say that the Capulet Montague fight is over now.

But nothing will ever bring back Romeo and Juliet.

The saddest loss of all. 💔

Send

Romeo and Juliet are in a relationship.
 For eternity.

👍 140 likes   REPLY

Capulet: Cheers! 🍷🍷🍷
Lady Capulet: Oh, honey! So happy for you. 🤍
I hope you wore white. Love, Mom.
Montague: I ordered a gift from the registry.
Should be there in a week. 😃
Benvolio: Congrats! You guys were always my
favorite couple.
Nurse: Aw, yeah! Get it, you two. #instalove

Send

The 411 for Those Not in the Know

411: Information

ASAP: As Soon As Possible

BB: Bye-Bye

BFF: Best Friend Forever

BRB: Be Right Back

BTW: By The Way

FML: F*ck My Life

FOMO: Fear Of Missing Out

G2G: Got To Go

GL2U: Good Luck To You

GTFO: Get The F*ck Out

IDGAF: I Don't Give A F*ck

IDK: I Don't Know

IDEK: I Don't Even Know

IMHO: In My Humble Opinion

IRL: In Real Life

Send

L8R: Later

NBD: No Big Deal

NP: No Problem

OMG: Oh My God

OMFG: Oh My F*cking God

SMH: Shaking My Head

STFU: Shut The F*ck Up

TBH: To Be Honest

TL;DR: Too Long; Didn't Read

TT4N: Ta Ta For Now

TTYL: Talk To You Later

TTYS: Talk To You Soon

TY: Thank You

WTF: What The F*ck

YOLO: You Only Live Once

Send

some emotions you might find in this book

😠 Angry

😣 Anguished

🙁 Confused

😵 Dead/Dying

😏 Devious

😞 Disappointed

😊 Embarrassed

😤 Extremely angry (fuming)

😭 Extremely sad (crying)

😘 Flirty

😉 Friendly (wink, wink)

😖 Frustrated

😜 Goofy

Happy

Indifferent

Love

Sad

Shocked

Shocked and screaming

Sick

Silly

Sleepy

Unamused

Worried

Zipped mouth

Send

BRETT WRIGHT has a BFA in creative writing and works full-time as a children's book editor in New York City. In college, he studied Shakespearean tragedy, which sadly lacking in emoticons. His greatest love affair has been with pizza. 🍕
@brettwright

WILLIAM SHAKESPEARE was born in Stratford-upon-Avon in 1564. He was an English poet, playwright, and actor, widely regarded as the greatest writer in the English language and the world's preeminent dramatist. His plays have been translated into every major language and are performed more often than those of any other playwright. 🎭

Send

FOMO?

Read on for a peek at

Laertes

And listen . . . there's something else I want 2 talk 2 u about.

ophelia

your excessive use of 2s???

Laertes

Ha. Ha. Ha. 😐

ophelia

i'm listening . . .

Laertes

I know u have been hanging out w/ Hamlet a lot lately. I just want 2 make sure you're not getting 😍. Sure he might say he 🤍 u now. But he's the prince. 🤴 His #1 priority is & always will b 👑. Please just don't get 😫.

ophelia

i know, i know. you have nothing to worry about.

Laertes

So you'll b careful?

Send

ophelia

i have 🔒 your words in my 💚 and you alone have the 🔑. but it goes both ways. you better stay out of trouble in 🇫🇷!

Laertes

👍

● ● ●

polonius

Son, b4 u go, I made this 📝 for u.

◀ BACK	**POLONIUS**	+

Advice 4 Laertes on His Trip 2 🇫🇷:

1. B careful what u say. ⏱️👄

2. 💡 b4 u act.

3. B friendly, but not 2 friendly. 😉

4. Hold on 2 good friends 👬, but don't waste ur 💰💰💰 on every new person that comes into ur life.

5. Stay out of fights. But if u find urself in 1 anyway, kick some ***. 👊

Send

6. Listen 2 every1, but don't waste ⏰ & energy on ppl who don't deserve it.

7. 👀 what other ppl do, but don't 👮 them.

8. Dress nicely, but don't go overboard. (u know how 🎩 ppl are.) 🎩 👔 💼 🪒

9. Don't borrow or lend 💰 2 friends or u might lose both. And/or u might start 2 resent them. And/or they might start 2 resent u! 😠

10. Above all: b true 2 urself. If u are completely urself, then u 🚫 b fake 2 any1!! ⭐

Laertes

Thx, Dad. I'll let u know when I get there. 😎

Polonius

Good luck! 🍀

Group text: Laertes, Ophelia, Polonius

Laertes

About 2 board. Bye, guys. Ophelia, remember wut I said!! 🔒

Send

ophelia

xoxo

● ● ●

polonius

U can tell me what that was about when I get 🏠.

ophelia

sigh. if you must know, it was about hamlet.

polonius

I knew it. U 2 have been spending a lot of ⏰ 2gether. What's going on? & ⚠️ don't u dare lie 2 me!

ophelia

dad, it's just . . .

he 🏹 me.

polonius

He probably 🏹 CANOODLING w/ u!

Send

ophelia

ew. dad. please don't ever say something like that again.

polonius

Don't b naïve. He's the prince! Do I need 2 make U a  of advice like ur brother?! That's it. U r forbidden 2 speak 2 Hamlet ever again. 😶

ophelia

dad, stop. you're overreacting. he's serious about me. 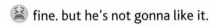 soon?? 😉

polonius

You rly don't have a choice. This ends NOW, Ophelia.

ophelia

😫 fine. but he's not gonna like it.

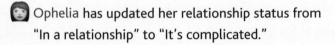 Ophelia has updated her relationship status from "In a relationship" to "It's complicated."

Send